Swing

Swing CAFE

STORY CARL NORAC ILLUSTRATIONS REBECCA DAUTREMER
NARRATION BEBEL GILBERTO & DAVID FRANCIS

A swinging cricket's biography, based on the unpublished
memoirs found on a jacaranda leaf.

Any resemblance to the life and dreams of Zaz,
born under palm tree number 112 on the half-moon beach
Princesinha do Mar in Copacabana, is not a coincidence.
After all, she's the story's hero.

Somewhere in the far reaches of Brazil, a cricket sleeps under a guitar.

Her given names are Esperanza Carmina Belleza. Her last name, well, let's not even go there. Everyone calls her Zaz, it's shorter, and has a nice ring to it. Down here, those three letters can be found written in the sand and on stones, and even in the smallest of clouds. There's not a single insect around that doesn't truly love her. When Zaz meets up with fleas, they are always after her for an autograph. "Not now little ones, *pequenas pulgas*," she croons. Of course, she's stunning: she has beautiful piercing green eyes, her wings are amazing.

But more than anything, Zaz can sing.

They say only male crickets can do it. ✪ Mesma coisa, sempre !

When she lifts her voice, plants bloom. The ocean waves softly clip and clap. Without there being any wind, shutters on houses flip and flap, playing conga drums to her song and dance. Zaz's voice wafts out like a perfume. Only praying mantises don't like Esperanza Carmina Belleza. For them, she's just too much, way over the top.

Beneath her diamond wings, Zaz has an angel's voice. But even with all the applause, the bright lights, the enthusiastic encores, something is missing in Zaz's life. "You can't live dreaming about another life," she keeps telling herself, as she watches the moon travel across the sky.

"I'm just a cricket. ★

My dreams are much bigger than my wings. The ocean, I shall cross. The ocean is no bigger than a tear. And my wish is to laugh above every wave. Here, Miro watches over me, a dear friend who's as sweet as candy.

We met on a grey afternoon. He was a butterfly who had lost all hope. He landed near me and looked at my shoeless feet. Without a word, he understood that I needed to leave for America and live out my dream.

The others always say, 'You're too young! Stay home, tucked in warm in the comfort of your matchbox. Aren't you happy under the palm tree?' But what's the point of having wings if you don't travel?

Sure, I've tried all sorts of odd jobs: eyeglass cleaner, tap dancer, makeup artist for birds, web mender for fashionable spiders.

The only thing I've never been able to do is say goodbye. I need to leave Miro for good. I have to speak to him about it. I practise in front of a water drop mirror. I say 'Tchau. 'Brigada meu amor. Te vejo logo, já, já.' But never goodbye, that simple little word. I just can't get it out.

Here comes Miro. I forget about what I want to say. He tells me that he's found a treasure. He takes me to a spot full of people. There's Jimmy, that oh-so-conceited flea, Anna, the firefly who's convinced she's the brightest star in the universe, and some young ants, proud as peacocks, who shout out, 'It's called a radio, it took the whole class to lift it up! There were five thousand of us!'

Miro elegantly bows to me, and then presses a button on the radio. It cracks like a ton of twigs, it starts shooting sparks. We all think it's going to blow up and then, and then, there is the most fabulous music!

Our legs are numb from so much dancing, and my wings are killing me, too. Miro lifts the little leaf that he wears as a cap to say 'see you later.' His eyes gleam like two small pearls. Tomorrow, I'll tell him everything."

Zapa-daza-zoo,
Zaz is on her way
to the U S of A!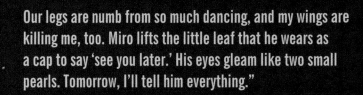

Zaz needs to be there to hear that music up close, while she still has time. Lay her wings down, and make her voice shine.

It's cold tonight. ★

Zaz, on the street Rua da Fonte, lays herself down on a poet's eyelid. She warms up and begins to play her secret game. She closes her eyes, sings softly, and suddenly the dreams of the insects around appear to her like paintings.

Close by, a little flea sees himself all snuggled up in his mother's hood. For their part, a few flying ants have night-mares of being grounded. A bee pictures herself in a vast palace of honey. Sometimes, Zaz sets these scenes to music.

Everything she hears, those strange or soothing sounds, she slips under her wings, and all the notes come out dancing on the edge of her dreams.

A bumblebee whistling joyfully in front of a cloud, a fly trying to purr, two butterflies stroking each other's wings like velvet cymbals, a mosquito convinced his stinger is a trumpet. All of it builds into a melody, just after midnight. Then, of course, still singing softly to herself, she falls asleep.

It's morning. ✪

Zaz awakens with a pearl of dew, already bursting with sunshine, on the edge of her nose. Stretching out, she makes up a new song. You would think, as strange as it may seem, that every grain of sand was listening to her.

It's now or never. Zaz is heading for New York. She'll just have to find a way. She feels that the time is right, and flies off to tell Miro. Wherever she ends up, he'll always be dear to her. But where is he hiding? At this hour, he should be on the pier. He always says he counts the waves and teaches the fish how to swim.

Miro fell in the flowers, his wings still beating. He didn't get back up. ⭐

The life of a butterfly like him only lasts a summer. Just enough time to make the lives of those around him brighter.

"I always knew it, but to make him laugh, I would draw him in the sand with a beard longer than he was."

Insects came, with small bouquets of grass. They set Miro down on the first wave of the morning, the one that goes out the furthest.

The sun came near and cast its light upon him. I cried out, "Look!"

After that, she couldn't speak. In unison, the bumblebees and the grasshoppers sang out to the open sea to wish him a good journey.

"*Tchau meu irmão. Adeus.*"

Like a captain without a compass, Miro took wing. He must be up there now, tucked in a secret corner of the sky.

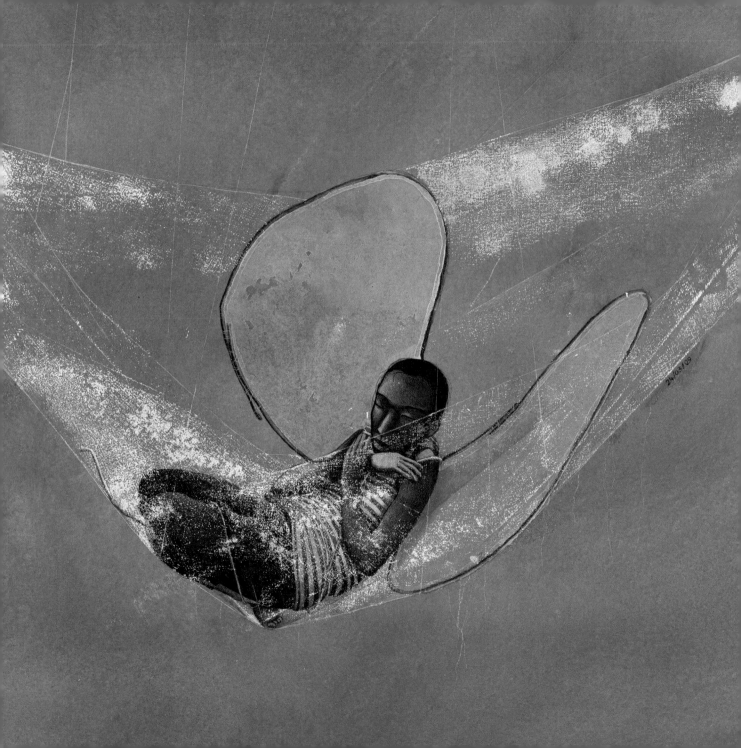

CHAPEÚ
Senhoras

Zaz noticed that the chic ladies buy hats just before taking the boat to New York. "If I hide in one of them, I'll get there," she tells herself. But which one? The round one? She'll be like a merry-go-round that's going too fast in there. The feathered one? It will make her sneeze. And the one with the needles is way too scary. Then, she notices the flowered hat.

A young woman is buying it right now, just before boarding. Zaz hides in its garden. The petals smell like paper.

But oh, what style! ✦

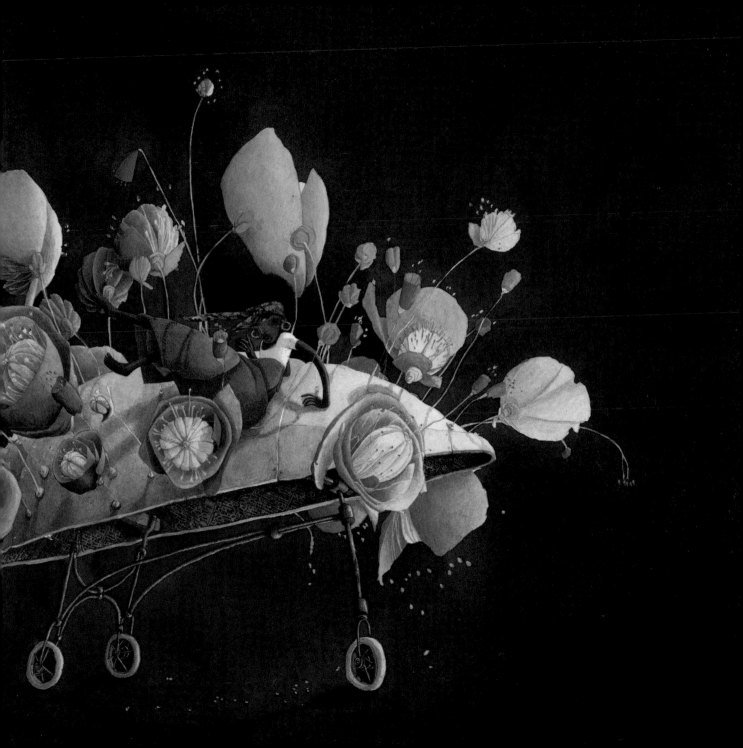

On the ship,
Zaz keeps still. ★

She's afraid the girl might smell her honeydew perfume.
At night, when a star trails the sky, Zaz's thoughts
turn to Miro.

"Welcome to New York! Climb on in!" says a taxi driver to
the young woman. "What a lifelike hat you have, the flowers
seem in full bloom, and that insect appears to be alive!"

The young woman howls. Zaz takes her leave by jumping
through the window. And suddenly, her joy takes flight.
Zaz is in Chinatown, and for her, this is America:
the colourful clothing, the hustle and bustle of the crowd,
the happy laughter and, most of all, the music pouring
out on every street corner.

All of a sudden, the rain comes down, enough to make the skyscrapers cower. Soup bowls become lakes, and the mud rustled up by stamping feet splashes on Zaz's cheeks. The music is drowned out by the rain's thump and blow. On the sidewalk, she sees people waiting in line just to get a piece of bread. She lands on the hand of a little girl who, though she has nothing, gives her a smile.

Just for her, Zaz pretends to lift up a tutu to dance. She laughs as she twirls but, despite herself, she feels the cold. Moving on, Zaz wraps herself in a piece of green paper. She doesn't know it's a lost dollar bill.

"I've got clouds deep down in my heart," she thinks. ★

"How will I make a living?

I will have to dance in the streets just to survive. I pray to the sun, but he doesn't show. 'You're nothing but a lamppost from the sticks!' I shout at him. I find safe haven in an old tin can that smells like rusty sardines eaten by a friendless man. Rats are shooting dice with a piece of mouldy cheese. I wanted jazz, but I got the blues.

'Not much use crying in the rain,' a beetle tells me. When he takes off his shell to give it to me, I say, 'No thank you, *o meu amigo*, that's too much.' He insists. I accept. I put it on my back. The beetle walks away, just about as naked as a beetle can be.

All of a sudden, the little shell becomes my whole world. ✪

Insects watch me walk by. I stay hidden beneath it. It serves me well, this shell. Umbrella, bumper, surfboard for puddles. In a garden, I set it down; it becomes my island. Later, I hear a voice behind me. 'Sorry,' says the beetle, 'it was just a loan.'

I give him back his shell. He kisses my cheek. A beetle's kiss that goes 'splat!' I don't like it that much. Yet when he walks away, I wave goodbye. It's strange. I should be sad, losing my shell. But no, not even a bit. I understand now that I don't need it any more."

Whose voice is that? ✷

Is it the beetle's? Zaz sees no one, but she gives the world a smile. Now she hears it well, the music from her deepest dreams. She flits around in search of the sound. Too late to stop! She lands on a strange kind of person, a blue fly that's never even been to the sea.

"Oh, I'm so sorry, I hope I didn't hurt you," she says, staring at his wings. He looks as sad as a postman without a love letter. This guy needs to be shaken awake, to be hopped on with hope, to be stir-flyed. He doesn't look like Miro at all, except for the gentleness in his round eyes. What can we talk about? Música! Música!

"I know that you like music. Earlier on, you were the only one listening to me when I was hidden. I'm Mister Buster, masked singer, as shy as a winter sun."

"So you're the one with the beautiful voice. Bravo, my friend! Do you know of a place around here where one can sing without a mask, and feel completely free?"
"At the Swing Café, a jazz club for dreamers.

It's much further that way, but shush! We can't say a word about it."

"Not a problem, since we're going there!" Zaz shouts.

Buster protests that the rain will dampen his wings, making the flight dangerous, and that he might even catch a cold. So Zaz decides to teach him the sport in which she excels: racing between raindrops. On your mark, set, go: she flies through lines of people, chins and moustaches, she jumps up on an elastic earlobe or a shoulder. Buster is running out of breath. The rain splitches and splatches. Zaz, feet in the water, feels for the puddles' sounds. She plays the drops and drums. She lands on a policeman and plays the banjo on his eyelashes. He tries to whistle and stop her. Too late, she has already moved on. He turns red with anger and calls her a wasp. She sticks out her cricket tongue and speeds off.

It jumps and jives, it turns and twists, it calls and falls and gets back up. It cries and flies and makes itself heard. It's noisy and nosy and way too racy. It shines and blinds and makes it shout. It pulls, it pushes and goes all about. It zigs without the zag, and zags after that. It's the Zaz dance, and it's about all that.

Buster calls out the path to take. He takes a bad turn trying to catch up, turns his twist and sprains his wrist.
He sits down and refuses to go on. "Come on," Zaz shouts, "Move! You're just like my old grandpa! He was the naptime champion. A century without moving, that was his secret dream. One day, I think he decided to die just to beat his record. Now's the time to get up and fly!"

Then, the storm hits. Its voice is heard, it can't be misunderstood. The Great Big Everywhere goes black. The Swing Café is much too far. Buster pulls Zaz towards his house, which is right beside them.

"I promise it's not to give you a kiss," he adds. His house proudly carries a name: Jazzy. When the doors open, it creaks jazzy. The dancing cardboard windows make a sound that's jazzy, jazzy. Even the polished floorboards squeak jazzy. Zaz laughs.

It's quite delightful, but not for long. Too light, the little place is lifted away by the wind. Before you can say jazzy three times, it's gone. Buster takes her to a safer place: the Store of Unsellable Things. A jungle of junk, it's easy to hide there.

A gust of wind, and you're in. ✹

Zaz finds a tone-deaf music box and dances without a sound. Her wings rustle up a crowd of dust. She finds all sorts of hidden treasures at the Store of Unsellable Things: 'Two-person magic broom for romantic witches'; 'Do-nothing machine (used)'; 'One-of-a-kind refrigerator (made to keep snowmen all year long)'; 'Self-walking boots, for those who've lost their way'; 'Not-too-strong castle, for not-too-mean warriors'; 'Cloud pipe, used by the ancients for dreaming.' Inside, there's still a bashful little piece of cloud. Just like Buster, but completely white.

Zaz just misses being pecked by the 'Parrot who bit his tongue while repeating sweet nothings.' He doesn't seem to want to say them anymore. Zaz pulls up her corset that he almost bit off and tells him: "Hey! No wonder you bit yourself, you fake romantic! Serves you right!"
"I found this for you," a proud Buster says.

'Pocket-sized bed, the ideal gift for tired ladybugs.'

"That's very nice, thank you. Tonight, I guess I'll be a ladybug." She lies down on its comfortably padded surface and falls asleep. Two hours later, she's awake from having too many dreams about the Swing Café. Among the torn posters in a corner of the store, she finds a photo of Carmen Miranda. Part singer, part fairy, she wears a pineapple in her hair. She's a bit like Zaz, in a non-crickety sort of way. Zaz makes herself a few fruits out of paper and mimics her. And then, she sees it: 'Gap-toothed piano, designed to play every second note. That's quite enough. A piano just for Zaz. She doesn't even know how to play.

Now, let's dance!" ✪

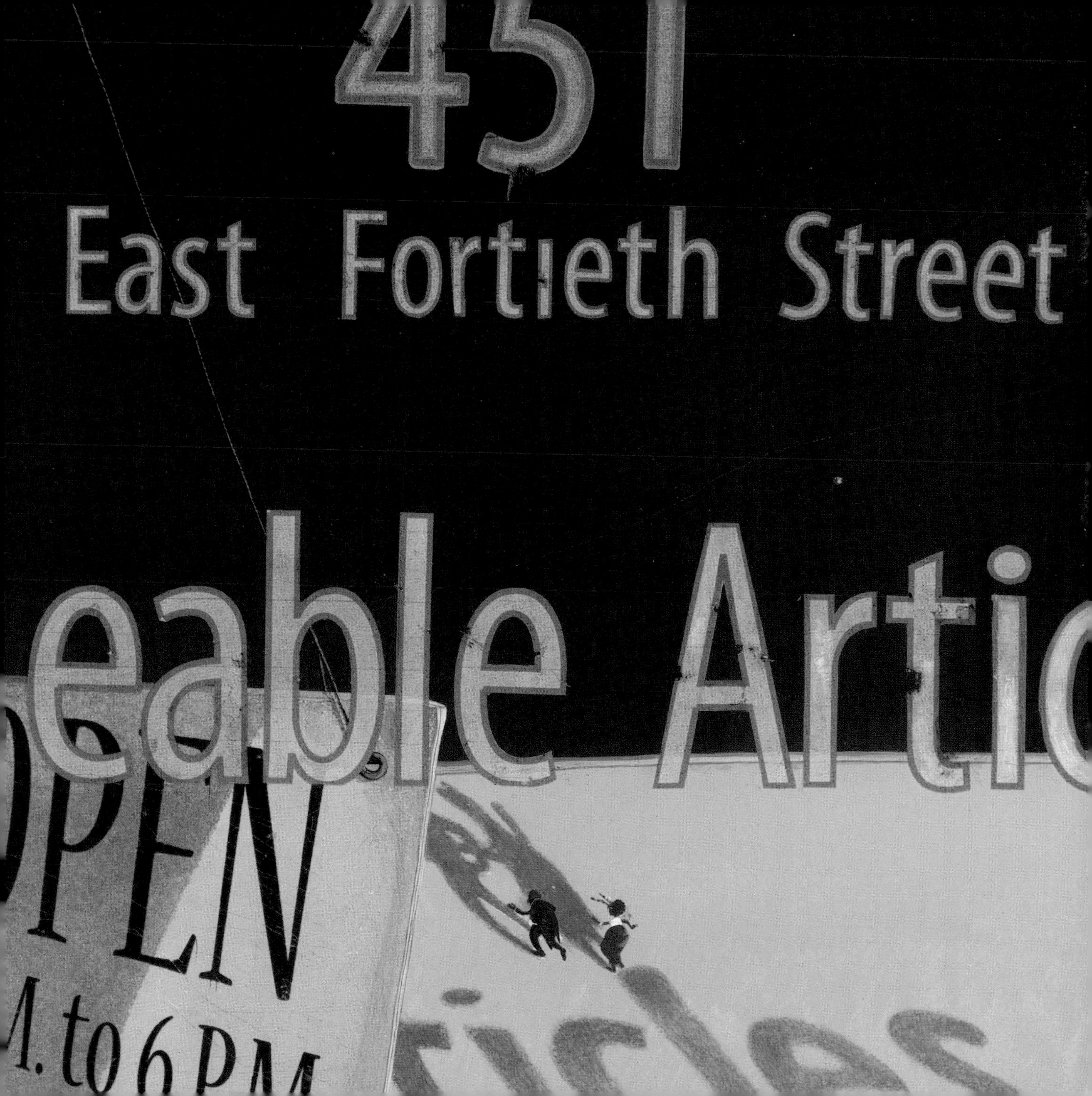
451
East Fortieth Street
eable Artic
PEN
M. to 6 PM

Zaz is making more noise than a handful of keys. ✦

"Awake now, the manager of the store arrives. He blames the parrot who, miffed, shows his chain. Then he sees me and grabs one of the items: 'Fly swatter with holes (to give one last chance).' Oh, that's not the way I want to end. I imagine the story that will be written about me: "Zaz, born near the sun, songstress from the stars, has died, squashed by a plastic fly swatter." I soar, I swirl, and I swoop. Anything to save my cricket skin. The store manager is getting worked up as I loop around his nose and then do an about-turn. Really, I'm just making things worse.

Buster pops up to save me. He shouts, 'Exterminator! Insect hater! Cricket swatter!' By the time the manager's asked himself how a fly can speak, we've slipped out under the door."

That's all, folks!

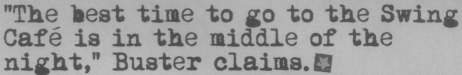

"The best time to go to the Swing Café is in the middle of the night," Buster claims.

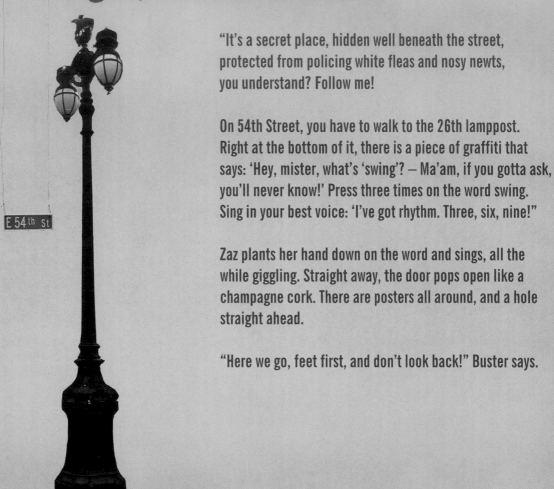

"It's a secret place, hidden well beneath the street, protected from policing white fleas and nosy newts, you understand? Follow me!

On 54th Street, you have to walk to the 26th lamppost. Right at the bottom of it, there is a piece of graffiti that says: 'Hey, mister, what's 'swing'? – Ma'am, if you gotta ask, you'll never know!' Press three times on the word swing. Sing in your best voice: 'I've got rhythm. Three, six, nine!'"

Zaz plants her hand down on the word and sings, all the while giggling. Straight away, the door pops open like a champagne cork. There are posters all around, and a hole straight ahead.

"Here we go, feet first, and don't look back!" Buster says.

E 54th St

faster, almost at a train's pace!"

Welcome to the Daybreak Express!

The slide is lit up by sparks. Shuffle, shuffle, groans the
tunnel as they hurtle through. "At the tunnel's end, there
are two paths to choose from. I take the wrong one.
Buster disappears.

In the darkness, I fall. ✳

There's a horrible noise, an off-key sound. I struggle, I'm a
prisoner. What is this? Slowly I start to see, as if a candle
was lit in my head. I am stuck between a banjo's strings.
Oh, this is terrible! *Que miséria, que horror !*

I'll pull on them and free myself.

Here, nobody knows just yet what Esperanza Carmina
Belleza is made of."

One great leap, and
Zaz smoothes out her wings.

Then she walks through a long room that smells of
smoke. In the furthest corner, there is an old curtain.
Little glow-worms spell out two words: Swing Café.

Not a note can be heard. You could hear a dustball fly
across the room. Is it closed? She slowly grasps the curtain,
then pulls it open in one swift movement.

Zaz whistles and claps.

There's not even time to say oo-bop-she-bi-boo-bop:
everyone wants to talk to her. Strange words tumble out,
faster than the speed of light. "What d'ya like to dance, do
you Scraunch, Lindy Hop, Charleston, Shimmy or Skeedle
Loo Doo?" "Can I be your hoochie coochie man, my sweet
patootie?" "Don't listen to that snookie acting the jazzbo
with his stovepipes and his zoot suit coat!"

"You're beautiful, bear cat, like a dollop of cream in a cup
of coffee! Come dance the Mooch so we can smooch,
Tee Nah Nah."

Zaz backs up and cries, "Leave me alone now! I don't
speak swing!" Ah! Now everyone wants to teach her.

"Don't say goodbye, say toodle-oo and come with me
on the Chattanooga Choo Choo." "Don't waste time
saying: 'How I am filled with joy and glee,'
all you have to say is, 'Whoopie!'

Mo Moocher, the singer, chases away the onlookers and begins to perform the Cakewalk. It's a way to walk just like the white flies, with a bow, a click of the tongue, a mocking look. He splits through the crowd and then turns serious and tells Zaz:

"We speak jungle so that we don't talk ghetto. It's true, we talk too fast, but there's no time to waste. Life is gone in a wink; don't miss it. At the Swing Café, we talk this way to get away from always saying ' yes, yes,' and to protect ourselves. A bit like a shell, you know what I mean?"

You bet!

Mo offers her a drink in a bottle cap, and introduces his musicians. On bass, a spider twangs his web. On trumpet, a smiling weevil; he really doesn't look that mean. At the piano, Duke, a very rare kind of grasshopper who tickles the ivories and teases the scales. On sax, a mosquito; he might look old, but every one of his notes is gold. On drums, the only bee who can't stand flowers; but when she hits the skins, she whips the air and makes pure honey.

"And you, Zaz, what do you do?" Mo asks. Not knowing why, she shakes like a leaf that's seen a caterpillar.
She whispers, "I sing," pulling her shadow around her.

"Buster is there.
He gives me a wink. ✶

His eyes light up with a smile. I'm not so afraid.
Just then I think I see Miro, at the edge of the crowd.

His loopy smile, his heart overflowing like a wave, Miro,
my little whirlwind, my dear, dear brother. I don't have to
go looking in other people's dreams anymore. I take the
little leaf that Miro wore on his head and that I secretly kept
with me, song to song. I hold it close to my heart. I snap
my fingers and I approach the thimble that doubles as a
microphone."

Don't expect a broken whimper. Zaz is a cymbal-smashing
cricket. You'll be hearing her soon! She has a transparent
body, so you will be able to see the beat of her heart.

"Right now, I am swing."

"Are you listening to me? Don't ever forget where the secret place is. Walk to the 26th lamppost on 56th Street. Right at the bottom of it, there is a piece of graffiti that says: 'Hey, mister, what's swing? — Ma'am, if you gotta ask, you'll never know!'

Press on the word 'swing,'
then slide right down,
I'll be waiting for you."

Featured recordings

1 **Manuello**
Performed by Carmen Miranda, Discograph, 1942
Written by Jack Yellen and Sammy Fain, EMI Feist Catalog

2 **Hot and Bothered**
Performed by Duke Ellington, Okey, 1928
Written by Duke Ellington, Mills Music

3 **Creole Love Call**
Performed by Duke Ellington, Gramaphone, 1927
Written by Duke Ellington and Billy Strayhorn, Mills Music / Campbell Connelly

4 **Tiger Rag**
Performed by The Mills Brothers, Brunswick, 1938
Written by James La Rocca and Larry Shields, Alfa Film Music

5 **Chinatown, My Chinatown**
Performed by Slim and Slam, Vocalion, 1938
Written by Chet Atkins, Jerome William and Jean Schwartz, Athens Music

6 **Shakin' the African**
Performed by Don Redman, Brunswick, 1931
Written by Ted Koehler and Harold Arlen, Mills Music

7 **Jivin' the Vibes**
Performed by Lionel Hampton, RCA Camden, 1957
Written by Lionel Hampton, Swing and Tempo Music

8 **Handful of Keys**
Performed by Fats Waller, HMV, 1937
Written by Fats Waller, Anne Rachel Music

9 **Daybreak Express**
Performed by Duke Ellington and His Orchestra, HMV, 1933
Written by Duke Ellington, American Academy of Music

10 **A Bunch of Rags**
Performed and written by Vess L. Ossman, Frémeaux & Associés

11 **Minnie the Moocher**
Peformed by Cab Calloway, Brunswick, 1931
Written by Cab Calloway, Clarence Caskill and Irving Mills, Mills Music

12 **Sing Me a Swing Song**
Performed by Ella Fitzgerald, Frémeaux & Associés
Written by Stanley Adams and Hoagy Carmichael, Peermusic

Recordings repeated in their entirety after the narration at the end of the CD:

13 Hot and Bothered 3'20
14 Creole Love Call 3'17
15 Tiger Rag 1'47
16 Chinatown, My Chinatown 2'41
17 Shakin' the African 2'44
18 Jivin' the Vibes 2'26
19 Minnie the Moocher 3'12

Story by **Carl Norac** translated by **Jacob Homel**
and revised by **Services d'éditions Guy Connolly**

Illustrations by **Rébecca Dautremer,** assisted by **Nejma Bourouaha,**
with documents borrowed from the audio-visual department of **the Bibliothèque
nationale de France.** Graphic design by **Taï-Marc Le Thanh** and **Stéphan Lorti**
Narration by **Bebel Gilberto** and **David Francis.**
Produced by **Paul Campagne** and **Roland Stringer.**

ⓡ www.thesecretmountain.com
ⓒⓟ 2010 Folle Avoine Productions
ISBN-13: 978-2-923163-62-8 / ISBN-10: 2-923163-62-1
First published in French by Didier Jeunesse, Paris, 2009

Printed in L.Rex Printing Company Ltd.

Book printed in China by L. Rex Printing Company
CD manufactured in Canada by Cinram